THE IRELAND'S EYE
SEAGULL

Written by: Lisa Brady

About the Author

Lisa was born in Dublin and lives in a coastal town, she loves to read and write and has been creating stories since she was ten. When she is not writing she can be found walking her dogs. The Ireland's Eye Seagull will be her first published book.

Illustrations by Nina Mkhoiani

ISBN

978-1-7392987-0-8

 LisaBradyauthor

I could not have done this
without some very special people.
Thank you for all your help and guidance.
To my family, Eric and Natasha.

This copy of
The Ireland's Eye Seagull belongs to

....

....

....

Did you know?

Irelands Eye was named by Vikings.
Ey is a old Norse word for Island.
The stack is a free standing rock formation.
The Martello Tower is a defensive fort.
The Wren is one of Ireland's smallest birds.
In Ireland Robins are a sign of good luck.

The only way to enter the Martello Tower on Ireland's eye
is by rope through a window that is high above the ground.

Irelands Eye is the name of an island in Ireland.
It is home to lots of creatures.
The Ireland's Eye seagull sits up high
on his rock at the back of the Island.

He is carefree at sea living with his flock
on a rock known as The Stack.
At the tip top of the island he feels a strong breeze.

When the weather is cold,
he puffs up his feathers to keep nice and warm.

He likes to fly over to Howth.
Sometimes he catches the boat.

One of his favourite things to do
is steal fish and a chip or two.
His favourite time of year is summer on the pier,
Fish and chips galore!

He flies from the pier to Balscadden Bay,
where he checks out the caves and watches the waves.

Next is the Martello Tower,
which is always surrounded by flowers.

He flies to the harbour and catches a fish
from the sea but he still feels hungry.

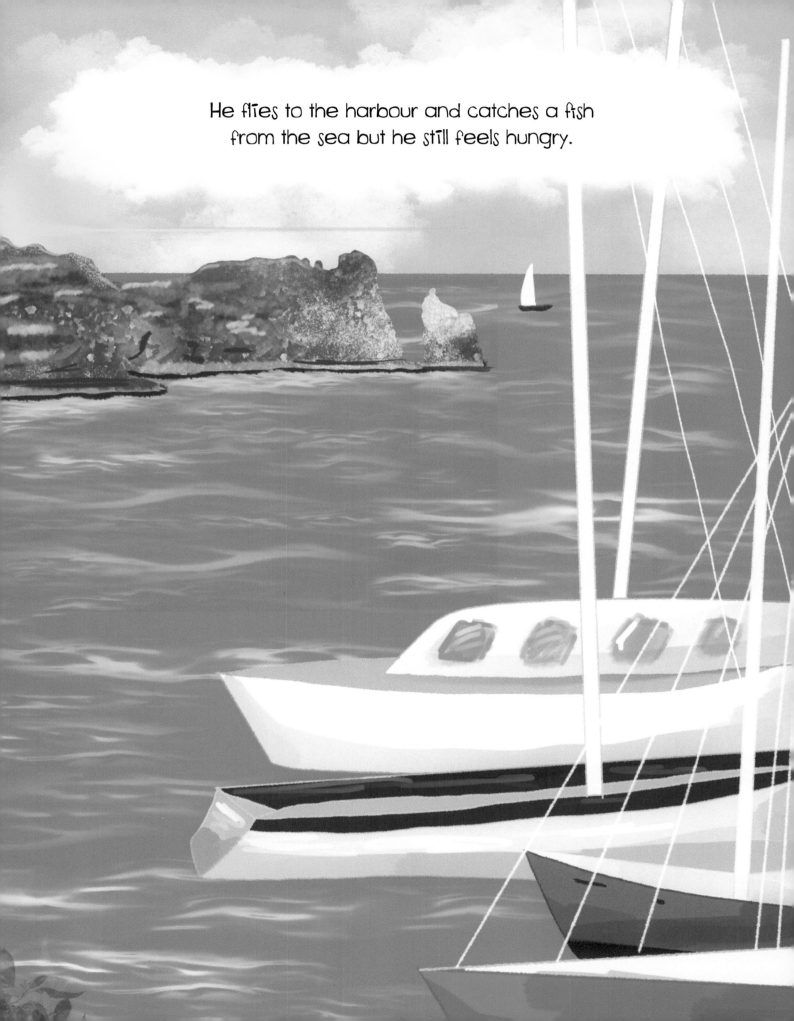

Then off to the summit of Howth
to look out at all the boats coming into Dublin Bay.

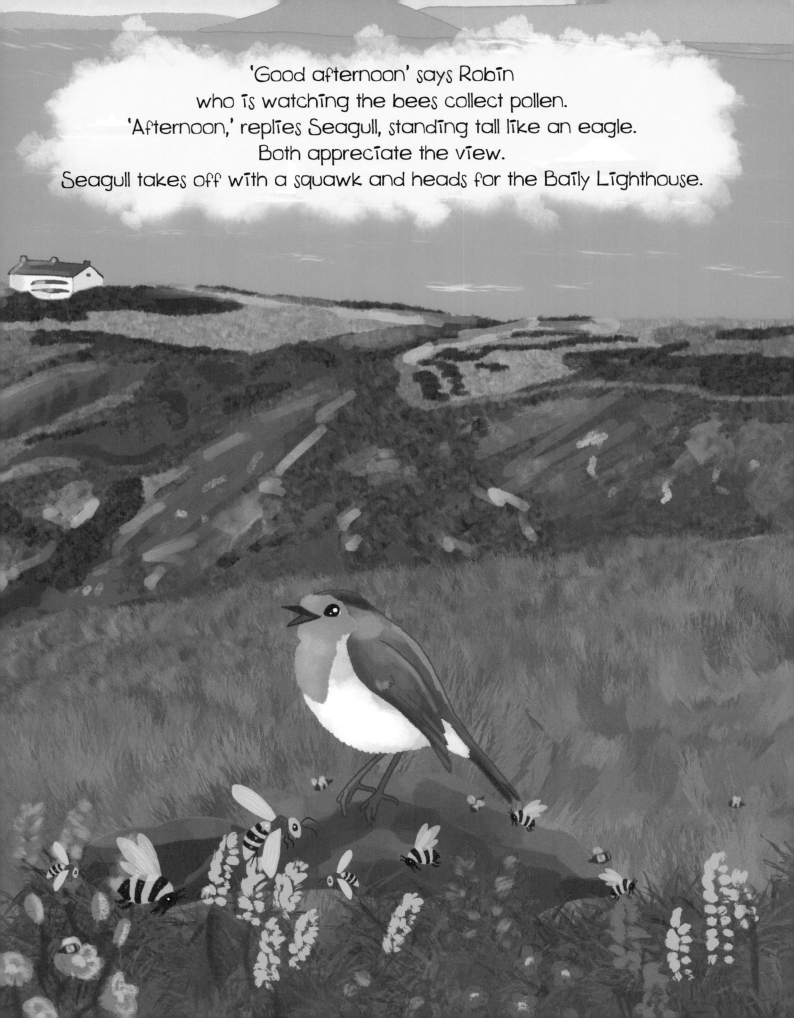

'Good afternoon' says Robin
who is watching the bees collect pollen.
'Afternoon,' replies Seagull, standing tall like an eagle.
Both appreciate the view.
Seagull takes off with a squawk and heads for the Baily Lighthouse.

He lands on the gallery next to a nice old man.
'Hold on,' said the man. Who ran and got his pan, holding it out to the bird.
'Fish fry,' the man says with a weathered smile on his face.
Seagull gulps down the food now in a great mood.

Then he takes off again for Howth Market.
He sits beneath a tent and watches everyone pass by.

Out comes a woman who knows him.
'I have something for you' she says.
It's some bread with a bit of spread. Seagull gobbles that up.
The woman goes back to the shops and Seagull begins to flop.
Boy, is he full!

He takes off again
and passes by a wren on his way back to the boat.

He lands with a thump onto the bridge
of the boat and makes the captain jump.
As they sail out of the harbour,
he is glad of the departure because he is very tired.

He gets a lift home, but flies the last part on his own.
He snuggles into his nest, ready for a rest.
He is carefree at sea, content and happy
while living with his flock on a rock known as 'The Stack'.

THE END